Published by Advance Publishers, L.C.
Maitland, FL 32751 USA
www.advancepublishers.com
Produced by Judy O Productions, Inc.
Designed by SunDried Penguin

Brother Bear
Printed in the United States of America

First published 2004.

A long time ago, when ice still covered the Earth, there lived three brothers in a small village, Sitka, Denahi and Kenai. One day, the villagers gathered for a ceremony where the village shaman, Tanana, presented the youngest brother, Kenai, with his special totem. It was a stone carved in the image of a bear. She said, "Your totem is love. Let love guide your actions." Years before, Sitka had received the eagle totem of guidance and Denahi had been given the wolf totem of wisdom. Kenai thought these were much better than the bear totem of love! Tanana gazed at the handprints on the cave wall and said, "One day you will place your mark next to those of your ancestors." But first Kenai had to learn to follow the true meaning of his totem.

That evening, there was to be a feast, so the brothers went to collect the fish they'd caught. But Kenai hadn't tied the fishing basket tight enough and a bear had stolen the fish in it. Angry, Kenai ran into the woods to find the bear. Sitka and Denahi followed and heard Kenai cry out. Racing to help their brother, they found him dangling from a ledge, trapped by the bear. While the three brothers tried to help one another, Sitka was cornered by the bear. To save his brothers, Sitka cracked the icy glacier and he and the bear plunged into the freezing water below. The bear fled, but Sitka was gone. He had lost his life to save his brothers.

Kenai was filled with rage. That night, he grabbed a spear and told Denahi they had to go after the bear. Denahi tried to stop him, but Kenai stormed off to track the bear alone. As he left, he threw his bear totem into the fire. Tanana quietly picked up the totem from the fire and gave it to Denahi. Kenai tracked the bear to a mountain top and the two fought until Kenai silenced the bear forever. Kenai let out a cry of grief, which Denahi heard in the distance.

Suddenly, blinding shafts of light surrounded Kenai. Animal spirits poured out of the light and the eagle spirit swooped down and turned into Sitka. Kenai was lifted into the air and transformed into a bear! When Denahi reached the mountain top, he found a bear standing on his brother's clothes. He didn't realize it was Kenai. Then a bolt of lightning struck the ground between them and Kenai was hurtled into the river below and swept away. Denahi swore revenge on the bear he thought had killed his younger brother.

Next morning, Kenai opened his eyes to find Tanana staring down at him. When he tried to tell her what had happened, Tanana said, "Kenai, I don't speak bear!" Kenai saw his reflection in the river and realized he was a bear! He ran around in a panic, growling and roaring – until Tanana hit him over the head with her shoe! "Listen to me! Sitka did this!" Tanana said. "I can't help you. Take it up with your brother's spirit! If you want to change, go to the mountain where the light touches the Earth." But Tanana vanished before Kenai could ask her how to get there.

Wandering through the forest, Kenai discovered he understood what other animals were saying! But when he asked for directions, they fled in terror. Kenai got caught in a bear trap and while he was dangling helplessly, a bear cub named Koda appeared and teased Kenai for not seeing the trap... The talkative cub told the irritated Kenai he was on his way to the Salmon Run. "How about this? I get you down – then we go together," suggested Koda. But stubborn Kenai refused and continued to struggle until Koda's constant chatter wore him down! Exhausted, Kenai agreed to Koda's request – and the cub helped him down with a CRASH!

Then Koda sniffed the air and started to race away. "Run!" he yelled, just as a hunter burst through the trees. It was Denahi! Kenai cried out, "Denahi, it's me – Kenai!" But Denahi didn't understand – all he heard were growls – and threw a spear at him. Kenai raced away and hid in an ice cave where he found Koda. While they hid, Kenai tried to back out of his promise to Koda, but the cub told him he'd lost his mother and the only hope he had of finding her was to go to the Salmon Run. "Please come," begged Koda. "Every night, we watch the lights touch the mountain." Kenai realized that Koda was going to the very place that Tanana had described – the place where he could become human again!

It wasn't an easy trip! Koda loved to chatter and play, and Kenai found this very annoying. But after a while, Kenai started to enjoy himself and Koda's bear ways. One night, while riding on the backs of mammoths, Koda and Kenai gazed up at the northern sky and talked about the spirits. Kenai said, "My brother Sitka is a spirit. If it wasn't for him, I wouldn't be here." Koda looked up at the stars and said, "Thanks, Sitka. If it weren't for you I'd never have met Kenai." The next day, they came to an abandoned village and saw cave paintings of a hunter and a bear. "Those monsters are scary," said Koda. Kenai had always thought bears were monsters but, as he held a paw up to a human hand, he realised Koda saw the humans as monsters. Kenai wasn't sure what he felt any more.

Koda and Kenai's adventures continued until they reached the Salmon Run. Koda was so happy and looked for his mother, but she was nowhere to be found. Kenai was terrified – he'd never seen this many bears in one place. But they welcomed him and soon he and Koda were having a wonderful time. That afternoon, the bears gathered to tell stories of the past year. As Koda told the story of his mother hiding him in bushes and being surrounded by humans, Kenai realized it was the story of the day Sitka had died – but now he knew it was also the story of a mother bear protecting her cub. Kenai realized Koda's mother was the bear he'd killed to avenge his brother's death!

Kenai wandered away feeling terrible! When Koda found him, Kenai explained what he'd done. Koda ran away in tears and Kenai, knowing he couldn't make up for what he'd done, decided to climb up to where the lights touched the Earth. But when he got there, Denahi was waiting and lunged at him. Suddenly, Koda came charging in and knocked Denahi over. Furious, Denahi chased after Koda. Then Kenai jumped to action and ran to protect the little bear from his brother. Then, just when it seemed as if there would be a terrible fight, a great eagle spirit appeared. He picked Kenai up off the ground and turned him back into a human!

The eagle turned into the spirit of Sitka. Kenai then looked behind a nearby rock where he saw a very frightened Koda. "Don't be afraid. It's me," Kenai said gently to the cub. Recognizing something in the human before him, Koda ran into Kenai's arms. Kenai realized how much the little bear needed him and how much he loved Koda. He knew he had to become a bear again. Sitka placed the bear totem around Kenai's neck, and Denahi turned to Kenai and said, "No matter what you choose, you'll always be my little brother." Sitka transformed him into a bear and turned himself into an eagle, and flew away into the magical lights.

Back in their village, Tanana greeted both boy and bears. She then made Denahi the new village shaman. Denahi then helped his brother bear place his paw print next to the hand prints of the villagers who had come before him. At last Kenai had learned to follow his totem. He had let love bring all his brothers together, both human and bear – for the rest of his days.

The End